A Frog Ate My Sandwich!

Written by
Christine Durkin

Illustrated by
Mousam Banerjee

This book is dedicated to my daughters, Brooke and Sara, without whose encouragement and support I would not have had the confidence or courage to publish. Special thanks also to my dear friend Dorothy, who supported my efforts all along the way.

"Finish your breakfast, Caden," called his dad. "The bus will be here soon!"
His dad was packing Caden's lunch for school, and today's sandwich was Caden's favorite -- cheese, lettuce and pickles. Caden could hardly wait for lunch!

As Caden finished eating his breakfast, he heard a weird noise. Then he heard it again. Caden looked up, and there, he saw a frog sitting right in his window!

When Caden looked at the frog, the frog looked right back at him and said, "Ribit, ribit."
"So it was you making that sound," Caden said, smiling.
The frog smiled right back at him!
He seemed really friendly.

"Let's go buddy; the school bus is here!"
his dad called again.
Caden knew he wasn't allowed to bring a frog to
school, but he really wished that he could.

"Will you wait here for me?" Caden asked the frog.
"I can't bring you to school with me, but I'll be back home
soon. Oh, and when I get back, I'll bring my best friend,
Nate. He'll want to meet you too!"
Then Caden waved goodbye to the frog, and walked out to
the door to the bus.
But this sneaky frog did not want to wait for Caden to
come back from school. He did not want to wait to meet
Caden's best friend, Nate. He wanted to go to school, too,
and he wanted to go now. So, while Caden was walking out
the door, the frog secretly hopped into his lunch bag.

When Caden got on the bus, Nate was already in his seat.
So Caden hurried to sit down next to him.
"Nate, a frog came to visit me when I was eating breakfast!
He was sitting in my window, and we looked at each other,
and he smiled at me. I swear! I asked him to wait for me, so
you could meet him when we got home from school!"
Then Caden heard that strange sound again.
Nate heard it too. "Ribit, ribit."

It was coming from Caden's lunch bag! Caden opened
the bag and both boys looked inside. There, they saw
the frog hopping around on Caden's sandwich!
He looked up at them and grinned.

"Oh, no! Now what do we do?" Caden asked.
"He must have hopped into my bag when I wasn't looking!"
Nate thought it would be cool to have the frog come along
with them to school. But Caden reminded Nate that the
school didn't allow that.

"Besides," Caden asked, "how can we hide a noisy, sneaky
frog, who keeps saying ribit, ribit all the time?"
Nate thought about that. "You're right Caden, that could be
trouble. Let me talk to him."

He looked down at the frog and said "Listen, frog, if you want to be at school with us, and you want to ride the bus back home with us, you need to be really, really quiet at school today; otherwise we'll all be in big trouble."
The frog looked back at Nate and blinked. Nate wasn't sure if that meant yes or no.

Then Nate turned to Caden and said,
"We can't just keep calling him frog. He needs a name."
Caden agreed, and started thinking about what they should call
him. "Oh, I know!" Caden said. "We could name him Walter.
Walter's my grandpa's name!" Nate thought that was a great
name for a frog, and so, Walter it was.

Soon the bus arrived at school, and both the boys and Walter went into the classroom. They were anxious to start the day, which promised a lot of fun projects, a great time at recess, and really cool science experiments and stuff. Plus, their teacher, Miss Zoe, was really nice.
The bell rang to say it was time for class to start, so both boys took their seats. They listened for Walter, but so far, Walter was staying quiet.

But sneaky Walter was curious about what happened at school, so he peaked out from the lunch bag. When he looked around, he got so excited about all the kids he saw in the classroom that he forgot to be quiet, and croaked, "Ribit, ribit," again!

Abi, the girl who sat next to Caden in class, heard Walter too. She looked over at Caden and asked, "What was that sound? It sounded kind of like a burp. Caden, did you just burp?"
But when she looked over at Caden, she saw Walter peeking out from his lunch bag instead.

"Ahh!" she gasped, and ran out of the classroom.
Miss Zoe, not knowing what had happened,
quickly went down the hall after her.

The yelling scared Walter so much that he crawled up Caden's pants leg to feel safe. It made Caden start wiggling around, so while Miss Zoe was out of the classroom, he quickly ran to the bathroom.

Once Caden was there, he shook Walter out of his pant leg. "Not cool, Walter," he said. "How can I bring you back in the classroom without everybody seeing you?" Then Caden had an idea.

"Okay Walter, this is our last chance. I'm going to put you under my baseball cap and you just need to be still until I get to my seat."

He carefully walked back into the classroom with Walter under his cap. Walter was trying to stay still, but he couldn't help moving a little, and that made Caden's hat start moving too.

Nate noticed and started giggling and Caden knew the other kids would notice a moving baseball cap soon too.

He quietly slid Walter back into the lunch bag and zipped it closed.

At last, it was time for lunch. The boys were pretty hungry, and couldn't wait to have their sandwiches now that Walter was finally being quiet. But when Caden opened his lunch bag, Walter was there, but Caden's sandwich was gone!

"Oh no!" Caden cried. "I think Walter ate my sandwich! Walter! Now what did you do?"

Then Nate started to laugh.
"Why are you laughing?" Caden asked.
"I have no sandwich!"
Nate said, "It's okay, Caden, I can share my
sandwich with you."

And then opened his own lunch bag.
"Let's see what kind it is."
When Caden looked inside, he saw Nate's sandwich,
but he saw his own sandwich, too,
right next to Nate's!

"How did my sandwich get in your bag?"
"I played a joke on you!" Nate said, laughing. "I wanted you to think Walter ate your sandwich, so I took it out of your bag and put it into mine to fool you!"

Then Caden started to laugh too. "That was funny, Nate!. But I'm so glad I have my own sandwich back!"

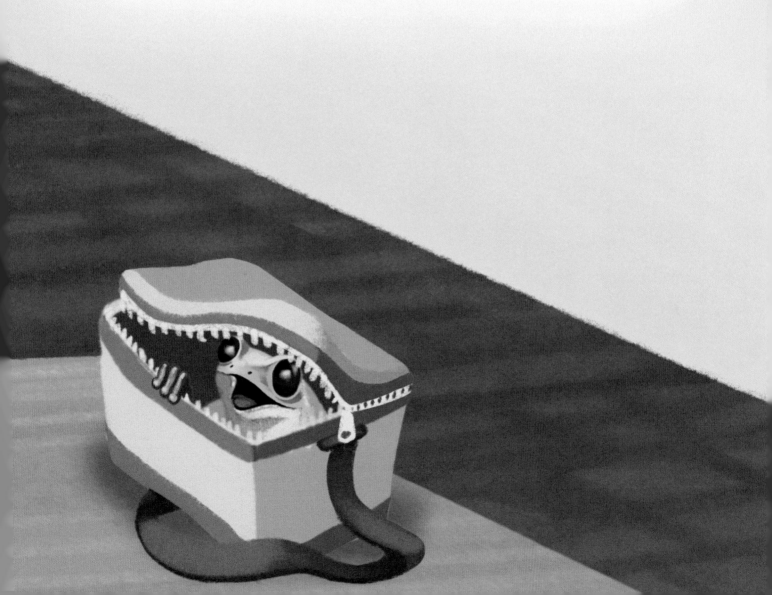

Soon the school day was over, and it was time to get on the bus to go home. Once they got back in their seats, they wanted to see what Walter was up to. He was still being really quiet. But when they looked in to check on him, Walter didn't look back up at them. He wasn't smiling, or hopping, or saying "Ribit, ribit." He looked really sad.

"I think he misses his family," Nate said. "I think he wants to go home." Caden was hoping to play with Walter and Nate once they got off the bus. He didn't want Walter to go back home. He wanted to keep him. But he didn't want Walter to be so sad. "You're right, Nate. I would miss my family too. I guess we shouldn't keep him."

Then Nate had an idea. "Maybe we should bring Walter back to your house. He jumped into your window, so he probably lives close by!"
Caden got excited at that idea. "Yes!" he cried out. "Maybe, then, he'll come back and visit us again!"

When they got off the bus, the boys went straight to Caden's back yard. They opened the lunch bag, and they let Walter out. He quickly started to hop, hop, hop away, toward his home.

As Nate and Caden watched him go, they knew
they would miss him. But they also knew that
Walter would be so happy to be back with his own
family. And knowing that made them glad too.

Walter kept hopping farther and farther away.
Then, suddenly, he stopped. He turned to look
back at the boys, smiled, and waved goodbye.

About The Author

Christine is a mother, grandmother and first-time author.
Recently retired from an advertising career, she's turned her
appreciation for the written word to writing books for children
that entertain while teaching life lessons.
She currently resides in Saint Augustine, Florida.

A Frog Ate My Sandwich is her first children's book.
You can reach her at oceanna@gmail.com.

About The illustrator

Mousam Banerjee is a full time artist and illustrator who loves painting whimsical children's
books to realistic concept art. Born in an artistic family, He was keen on creating original
paintings right from childhood. With a Post Graduate Diploma in Fine arts,
he now has made a full time career in Digital illustrations.

You can reach out to him at www.illus-station.com
or
www.instagram.com/illusstation.kids

"Hi Kids! Walter Here!"

I got in trouble again.
A LOT of trouble.

And it was SO. MUCH. FUN!!

It's all in my new book *Walter Hits a Home Run.*

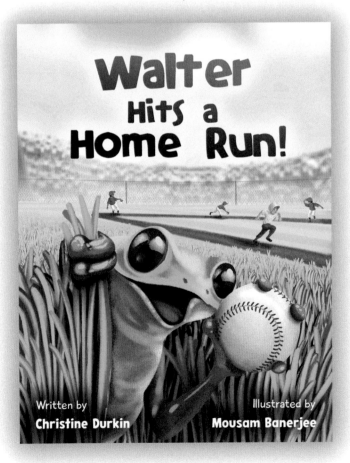

Walter Hits a Home Run!
Is book two in **The Adventures
of Walter the Frog** series.

Available now on Amazon.

Made in the USA
Coppell, TX
31 October 2024

39204024R00019